THIS
BOOK
BELONGS
TO
Mark
H.
Hedstrom

JOYCE WILLIAMS WARREN lives on Long Island with her husband and three young daughters. For several years, she taught English at Queens College, but is now a full-time doctoral student at Columbia University. She has published articles in literary journals, and writes a weekly environmental column for a local newspaper, but this is her first published work for children.

A Mouse
To Be Free

Joyce W. Warren

Illustrated by Jerry Lang

A CAMELOT BOOK / PUBLISHED BY AVON BOOKS

To my father —
 who gave me the little mouse
 and
To my mother —
 who gave me her love of all living things

AVON BOOKS
A division of
The Hearst Corporation
959 Eighth Avenue
New York, New York 10019

Text Copyright © 1973 by Joyce W. Warren.
Illustrations Copyright © 1973 by Jerry Lang.
Published by arrangement with Sea Cliff Press, Ltd.
Library of Congress Catalog Card Number: 73-83012.

ISBN: 0-380-00349-X

First Camelot Printing, August, 1975.

CAMELOT TRADEMARK REG. U.S. PAT. OFF. AND IN
OTHER COUNTRIES, MARCA REGISTRADA, HECHO EN
U.S.A.

Printed in the U.S.A.

The small nut-brown mouse
With pink ears and black eyes
Came out of his house
And looked up at the skies.

"Oh dear," said the mouse,
"I have very wet feet.
I hope it is drier
Down there in the street."

He looked to the left,
And he looked to the the right,
But his shiny black eyes
Saw no one in sight.

It had rained for so long
He was glad it was done,
For his fur felt so good
In the warmth of the sun.

But the grass was so wet
That it tickled his toes,
And he stepped in a puddle
Right up to his nose.

So he ran through the grass
On his quick little feet.
He stopped at the curb
And looked down in the street.

But what he saw there
Made his little nose quiver,
For right at his feet
Swept a fast-moving river!

He watched as the water
Swirled by at his feet,
And he wondered where he
Could find something to eat.

A stick floated by
And some paper and things,
A leaf, then an ant,
And some butterfly wings.

And floating along
In the watery gutter
Was a small piece of bread
With a smidgen of butter.

He reached for the bread,
But it floated on by.
The mouse lost his balance
And fell with a cry.

He splashed and he splattered
And paddled his feet,
And soon he was swimming
Down Sycamore Street.

He swam straight for the bread,
But just as he neared
The bread he was chasing —
It quite disappeared!

It was then that he heard it —
A fast, rushing sound —
And he swam for his life,
But he kept losing ground.

For there by the curb
Was a big sewer hole,
And the water rushed down
With a roar and a roll.

He tried to turn back,
But the current was strong,
And though he swam hard,
He was swept right along

To the big gaping hole
That had swallowed the bread,
Till, WHOOSH, in he went,
Like a child on a sled.

7

Down, down fell the mouse,
Spinning round and around,
To the depths of the sewer
Down under the ground.

He landed at last
With a terrible splash.
And he thought he would burst
From the force of the crash.

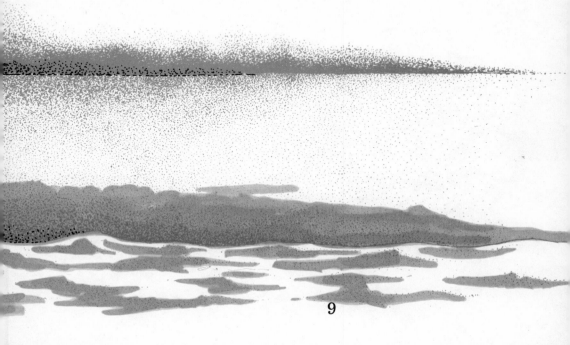

He was weak from the fall,
But he'd no time to rest,
For the water rushed on,
And he couldn't protest.

He had to keep swimming
Though weary and spent,
So on through the pipes
Of the sewer he went.

It was dark. It was cold,
And he felt so alone.
He was wet. He was frightened.
He wished he were home.

The sewer seemed endless,
And blacker than night,
Till he saw up ahead
Just the tiniest light.

He swam to the light.
It seemed only a dot.
But as he came nearer,
He saw it was not.

It grew and it grew
Like the sides of a funnel,
And he knew he had come
To the end of the tunnel.

13

"At last," said the mouse,
"I can see where I am."
And right to the edge
Of the sewer he swam.

The water rushed out
Like a dart from a bow,
And hurtled the mouse
To the river below.

He fell with a splash
That was worse than before,
And the water closed over
His ears with a roar.

Down, down he plunged
In the river so deep,
Down where the fish
And the mud turtles sleep.

He started to swim
When he felt himself stop,
But he thought he would never
Get up to the top.

Up, up he swam,
Not a moment to spare.
Then he burst to the surface
And gasped at the air.

When he got back his breath,
He looked up in dismay,
For the banks of the river
Seemed so far away.

He looked all around him
In search of a boat.
"I don't care what it is,
If it only can float."

There were sticks in the water
And bits of debris,
Leaves and old papers,
Some bark from a tree.

Then he saw up ahead
A matchbox afloat,
Just the size of a mouse,
And just right for a boat.

The box was half open,
The sides not too steep.
The mouse crawled inside
And was soon fast asleep.

Exhausted, he slept
As the day turned to night,
And the moon on the river
Shone silvery bright.

He drifted all night
In the little red box,
Past cities and farmyards,
And houses and docks.

Till just as the first
Morning rays of the sun
Crept into the matchbox,
His voyage was done.

He drifted ashore
In the fresh morning breeze,
And his craft was caught up
In the roots of the trees.

But the mouse was asleep
When the boat came to shore,
And he didn't awake
For an hour or more.

Then he woke with a start
And looked up in surprise —
Staring into the box
Was a pair of green eyes.

He trembled with fear,
For he felt certain that
Those glittering eyes
Must belong to a cat.

There was nowhere to run,
He was trapped in the boat.
And he wished he were still
On the river, afloat.

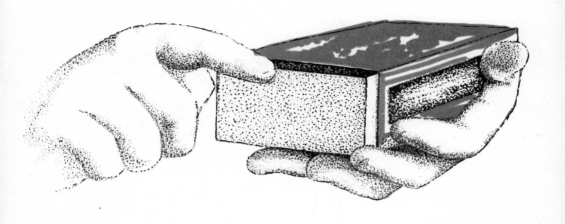

But just then the mouse
Heard a gentle voice say,
"Here Kitty, what's that?"
And the cat moved away.

And soon, where the cat
Had looked in at him, there
Were two big brown eyes
And some soft golden hair.

The box was closed gently
And raised in the air.
The mouse felt it moving,
But didn't know where.

He found himself placed
In a birdcage, alas.
The door closed behind him.
The bars were of brass.

A little girl stood
With her hand on the door,
While the black and white cat
Paced around on the floor.

"Don't be afraid,
Little mouse," the girl said.
"I'll bring you some cheese,
And I'll make you a bed."

"Poor Patty, my parakeet
Bird, flew away.
I don't need her cage
So you're welcome to stay."

Soon the trees were quite bare,
And the birds ceased their song,
While the wind whispered, "Winter
Will soon be along."

Then down came the snow,
And the mouse watched it storm,
So glad he was snug
In the house, nice and warm.

The winter was long,
And he watched the snow fall,
Till the black and white cat
Wouldn't go out at all.

So the cat stayed inside
With the mouse every day,
And they soon became friends
(Of a sort, anyway).

The cat curled up warm
By the fire's bright blaze,
And they talked and they talked
All those cold winter days.

Till the days had grown longer,
Snow melted away,
And the cat was impatient
To go out and play.

Then one day the cat
Didn't come for their talk,
And the mouse from his cage
Saw him out for a walk.

The window was open.
The air smelled so new.
It was spring. And the mouse
Longed to be out there, too.

The girl brought him cheese,
And she cleaned out his house.
But he just didn't act
Like the same little mouse.

He lay on his bed
And looked out through the glass
Where the black and white cat
Rolled around in the grass.

The sky was so blue
Over far away hills,
And the sun danced with joy
On the bright daffodils.

He ate almost nothing.
The days seemed so long
And the girl did her best
To find out what was wrong.

Each day when she brought him
A new piece of cheese,
He begged with his eyes,
And he tried to say, "Please,

"I am warm, I am fed,
With a house just for me.
But a mouse, to be happy,
Has got to be free."

Then one day she knew.
She could tell by his face,
As he watched through the window
A butterfly race.

"Do you want to be free,
Little mouse? Don't be sad.
I will soon set you free
Though it makes me feel bad.

"There are cats who can catch you,
And rivers so deep,
And you won't have a nice
Cozy bed when you sleep.

"There'll be no one to feed you,
To bring you your cheese."
But the mouse didn't answer.
His eyes still said, "Please."

So she took down his cage
On that very same day.
And she walked to the woods
That were not far away.

Then she set down the cage,
And she opened the door.
And the mouse darted out
On the green forest floor.

"Good bye, little mouse.
Please be careful," said she.
And he scurried away
To the side of a tree.

Then he stopped and looked back,
With his eyes shining now.
And he tried to say, "Thank you,"
But he didn't know how.

"I know there is danger.
I know it is hard.
But I'll be alert
All the time and on guard.

"For I have been down
In the river so fleet,
And I swam through the sewer
From Sycamore Street.

"I'll risk hunger and cold —
But I'd rather, you see.
For a mouse, to be happy,
Has got to be free."

Then he turned and he ran
Through the trees in the sun.
And he thought of the life
That he knew had begun.

So if ever you see
Such a little brown mouse
In the field or the woods
Or perhaps your own house,

Be as still as you can.
Take him quite by surprise.
And you may see the mouse
With pink ears and black eyes.

But don't try to catch him.
For, like you and me,
A mouse isn't happy
Unless he is free.